BAEP

Ink-blot

Library and Archives Canada Cataloguing in Publication

Eugenia, Maria, 1963-
[Mancha, a menina mal desenhada. English]
Ink-blot / Maria Eugenia.

Originally published under title: Mancha, a menina mal desenhada.

ISBN 978-1-927583-22-7 (bound)

I. Title. II. Title: Mancha, a menina mal desenhada. English

PQ9698.415.U54M3613 2013   j869.3'5   C2013-902532-4

First published in English in North America in 2013

Design by Jenny Watson

*Second Story Press gratefully acknowledges the support of the Ontario
Arts Council and the Canada Council for the Arts for our publishing
program. We acknowledge the financial support of the Government
of Canada through the Canada Book Fund.*

Printed and bound in China

Published by
Second Story Press
20 Maud Street, Suite 401
Toronto, Ontario, Canada
M5V 2M5
www.secondstorypress.ca

Ink-blot

Maria Eugenia

Second Story Press
www.secondstorypress.ca

Some people say
Ink-blot is
badly drawn.

Okay, we know that

most girls think...

they're
badly drawn.

Some worry

about
their
hair...

others about
their nose...

others about
their size.

Some worry
about everything.

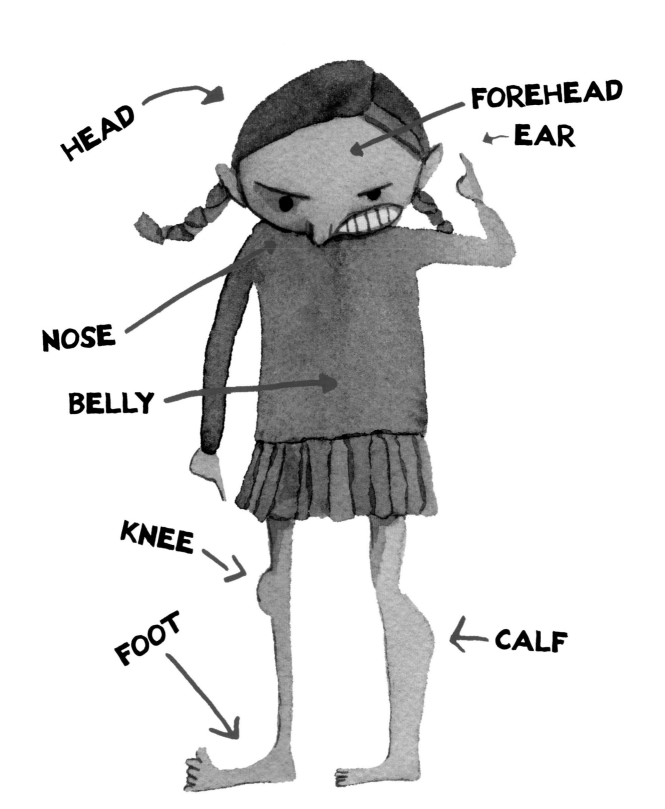

HEAD

FOREHEAD
EAR

NOSE

BELLY

KNEE

FOOT

CALF

Some even worry about

EARS

MONDAY

GLASSES

TUESDAY

FRECKLES

WEDNE

a different thing each day of the week!

That's a lot
of stress!

But, in Ink-blot's case, people say she really *is* BADLY DRAWN.

But, do you want to
know something?

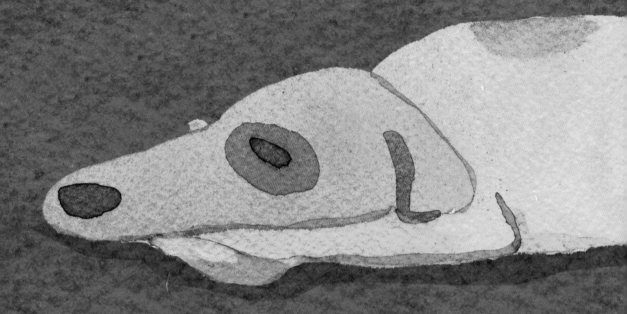

She's too busy having fun.

The END!